ROSIE F. SHANNON

The guardians of the Galaxy (holiday special)

Hot reviews and facts

This book is dedicated to the fans of Marvel

Contents

Introduction

The animated scene of a young Peter getting ready for the holidays with Kraglin before Yondu enters and destroys Christmas introduces the holiday special.

The Guardians of the Galaxy Holiday Special is arrived, and it's jolly merry! In classic Guardians of the Galaxy form, the plot twists and turns with laughter.

The movie was developed when Vol 2 was being made as the Marvel Cinematic Universe's first Disney+ release.

It was also shot concurrently with the impending Guardians of the Galaxy Vol 3, giving it an advantage to serve as a link between the events of Thor: Love and Thunder and the next picture.

The film also stands out for combining live-action footage with animation; in a recent Tweet, director James Gunn explained the inspiration for this intriguing decision.

The great hero Kevin Bacon is sent to Earth by Drax and Mantis as a Christmas gift for Star-Lord.

The bond between Mantis and Peter is further revealed, and this will undoubtedly be a moving story point in the future Vol 3. The story on Gunn's tenure and his current gangs of misfits will be closed in the future film.

The Cute and funny Gift from James Gunn

As a happy and lighthearted way to wrap up Marvel's Phase Four, James Gunn brings back the Guardians.

The 2022 film calendar is jam-packed with space-exploring superhero team projects, despite the fact that we haven't seen a new Guardians of the Galaxy movie in nearly five years.

In Thor: Love and Thunder, the Guardians already made a comeback this year, and the story of the first-ever roller coaster at EPCOT, Guardians of the Galaxy: Cosmic Rewind, is centered on this wacky team defending Earth.

The Guardians of the Galaxy Holiday Special is a wonderful lead-in to Guardians of the Galaxy Vol. 3 and a joyous way to wrap up Phase 4 and enjoy the holidays.

But in the five years since Guardians of the Galaxy Vol. 2 was released, there hasn't been a better reminder of why we love and admire these characters.

Peter Quill (Chris Pratt), who lost Gamora, is still in mourning in the Guardians of the Galaxy holiday special.

Quill's hero Kevin Bacon will be given to Quill as a Christmas present by

Drax (Dave Bautista) and Mantis (Pom Klementieff) in an effort to cheer up their boss.

Peter receives a Christmas he hasn't had since he was a boy when Drax and Mantis fly to Earth. They naturally don't quite fit.

Phase 4 has received a lot of flak for lacking focus, being disjointed, and having uneven quality.

The Guardians of the Galaxy Holiday Special, however, may have been a hit because writer-director James Gunn did not have to worry about creating a wider narrative or connecting it to a later film.

The Holiday Special might still exist, but in a bizarre form. Since these characters weren't as well-known back then, Gunn may have been less concerned with the team's wider ramifications; hence, it is comparable to what Gunn accomplished with the first movie.

Most Marvel films lack the freedom that is there in this one. This is a crazy, completely needless aspect of the Marvel Cinematic Universe, yet it only serves to make it more appealing.

The Guardians' two funniest members, Drax and Mantis, can also be highlighted at this point.

In their attempts to steal Kevin Bacon, they frequently veer off course. For instance, they might stop to chat with Avengers impersonators outside Grauman's Chinese Theatre or get too drunk at a gay bar.

The relationship between Bautista and Klementieff frequently causes others to laugh aloud when they are around this pair.

We previously knew that Drax was funny because of his dry sense of humor and inability to tell what tone was being used, but Mantis here really steals the show.

Mantis is always portrayed by Klementieff with the appearance that she is going to erupt in wrath; she frequently raises her voice in rage throughout a syllable, which is usually entertaining.

The fact that Drax and Mantis are confronting Kevin Bacon, a character from Peter Quill's past, and discovering that he is not the hero Peter thought he was, is also wonderful.

There is only one thing on the line in this Marvel project: Can these two characters abduct the Footloose star?

Kevin Bacon is enjoying himself while Drax and Mantis mock the actor and his films. Cosmo the Space Dog, a charming new member of our cast, is created by Maria Bakalova.

Cosmo doesn't get much of a chance to shine in the special, but it's already clear that the new Guardian will be a hit with viewers because this character is already so endearing, and Bakalova's portrayal just makes it cuter.

Regardless of The Guardians of the Galaxy, The modest size of this special adds to its delight.

The way this story is presented makes it seem quite warm and intimate, even though Mantis and Drax may be searching the universe for the ideal Christmas present.

In the emotionally charged sections of Holiday Special, the group is portrayed as a thrown-together family.

This connection works particularly well when Star-Lord has a chance to show his sincere gratitude for his comrades.

However, Gunn also demonstrates in The Guardians of the Galaxy Holiday Special how talented a storyteller he can be, given more creative latitude and lower expectations.

Even though we haven't seen him employ his skills in PG-13 content in a while, it still functions amazingly well. We've seen what he can do in the DCEU with fewer limitations.

It brings back thoughts of The Guardians' early days, when they weren't fully incorporated into the bigger MCU surrounding them, with his blend of wacky humor, a fantastic unconventional Christmas song, and emotional character moments.

The Guardians of the Galaxy Holiday Special, like the recently released Werewolf by Night, demonstrates how episodic specials can be just as powerful and brilliant as full-length Disney+ programs and Marvel Cinematic Universe films.

Volume 2 does a fantastic job of providing that while also generating anticipation for their return in Volume 3 next year.

This gang needed a quick reminder of what made these characters remarkable in the first place.

Featuring Gunn's masterful blending of camaraderie, humor, and emotional moments, Gunn's special is a wonderful holiday present.

It is a wonderful reminder of how much we adore these characters.

Cosmo's significance in the Guardians of the Galaxy series from Marvel Comics

Cosmo, who is loved by everyone, appears in the Guardians of the Galaxy holiday special (as they should).

Guardians of the Galaxy Vol. 3 might feature the adorable space dog prominently because he was based on a real dog.

A brand-new (furry) fan favorite has emerged in the Marvel Cinematic Universe, and it is completely irrational.

With the release of the Guardians of the Galaxy Holiday Special, Cosmo the Space dog receives her due in the highest-grossing franchise in history.

This four-legged friend has been in the Guardians of the Galaxy franchise since 2014, but she is now poised to have a significant role in the next Guardians of the Galaxy Vol. 3 movie as well as future flicks.

Despite the fact that Cosmo canonically belongs to the male gender as designated in Marvel Comics, Howard the Duck (at the time portrayed by Seth Green) mistakenly misgenders her in the first Guardians of the Galaxy movie.

Benicio del Toro's character The Collector was licked by Cosmo. According to Gunn, Cosmo is now a female, and Maria Bakalova, who provided the voice for Cosmo in Borat 2, is portraying Cosmo in The Guardians of the Galaxy Holiday Special.

Cosmo's participation shouldn't come as much of a surprise because it was hinted at in the Special Presentation's marketing campaign and trailer.

Furthermore revealed at Comic-Con 2022 was Bakalova. She's hanging out with the Guardians, who've got a new base of operations in Knowhere, and you can see her here.

What is the background of Cosmo from Marvel Comics?

Comic book Cosmo was sent into space as a test subject for the Soviet Orbit Program (P).

While stuck on Knowhere, Cosmo came into contact with cosmic radiation, which granted him the ability of telekinesis.

We know that his MCU counterpart abides at least in part by this, because Cosmo uses her powers to transfer food to her lips.

Although it hasn't been verified, she could employ a universal translator to communicate with the other team members.

The Real Inspiration Comes from Cosmos

Gunn defended the decision to gender-flip Cosmo in a time when the MCU is under criticism from toxic fans for providing every hero with a female counterpart (we're looking at you, She-Hulk haters).

When Dan Abnett and Andy Lanning created the male cosmo for Nova Vol. 4 #8 in 2008, Laika, a real-life Soviet space canine, served as inspiration. Sadly lost in orbit, the 1957 Russian spacecraft Laika was never intended to touch down on Earth.

Despite the fact that the circumstances of her death were not made public until 2002, scientist Oleg Gazenko has already expressed remorse about it and recognized they didn't learn enough about animals in space to warrant her sacrifice.

Gunn stressed in a tweet dated July 2022 that converting Cosmo to a woman requires returning to the original story of Laika and the source material.

Even as recently as last year, the Marvel's Guardians of the Galaxy video game from Square Enix depicted Cosmo as a guy, albeit one who was in care of a litter of puppies in Knowhere.

The comic book Cosmo is known as the Chief of Security in the floating Celestial's brain. We don't learn anything about her position in the Holiday Special, but this might subsequently play a significant role in the story.

What will Cosmo encounter next in Guardians of the Galaxy Vol. 3?

Cosmo is no longer in The Collector's custody, so that is at least a relief.

She has been liberated from her prison since the Power Stone destroyed Tivan's collection in Guardians of the Galaxy, but other from a brief appearance in Vol. 2's credits, no information has been released regarding her location.

Because Nebula (Karen Gillan) casually says that the Guardians bought Knowhere from The Collector in a line, it's likely that all of The Collector's exhibitions have been made public.

Despite the fact that it hasn't been proven that she is a Guardian, she seems at home among them.

As she was regularly included in the Guardians' issues, Comic Cosmo may help in introducing newbies like Moondragon or bringing back the "original" group that was lost after being hinted to in Vol. 2.

We have been informed that Guardians of the Galaxy Vol. 3 will be the final movie in the current lineup, yet this doesn't mean the Guardians franchise is gone.

After then, a lot of the characters could opt to stop acting or possibly pass away.

In the comics, Cosmo was tasked with forming the Annihilators as the team the Guardians should have evolved into when Star-Lord passed away.

In the event that Chris Pratt's Star-Lord is no longer alive, the story may continue, introducing significant figures like Beta Ray Bill and the Silver Surfer.

When two other humanoid animals on the team learn what Cosmo's future holds, Rocket will no longer be the most attractive.

Rocket won't be thrilled about this. Cosmo is a formidable figure in the comics who has already defeated Adam Warlock by himself.

Given that Will Poulter has been chosen to play Warlock in Guardians of the Galaxy Vol. 3, it would be exciting to see whether she has the abilities to extract a piece from him like she was Old Yeller.

It's not all belly rubbing and long walks, though, because Chukwudi Iwuji's High Evolutionary serves as the volume 3's primary opponent.

The High Evolutionary likes to use animals as test subjects, thus Cosmo and Rocket could be in danger.

With her drooly nose and waggy tail, the newest lovely girl in the Marvel Cinematic Universe isn't afraid to win over admirers.

Guardians of the Galaxy Holiday Special breaks the MCU's (Marvel Cinematic Universe) canon five times.

The Guardians of the Galaxy Holiday Special deviates from several established plot facts while adhering to MCU continuity while being a solo story.

The Guardians of the Galaxy's holiday special Is it a canon?

Although it is also recognized as a stand-alone Marvel narrative, James Gunn argues that it acts as the MCU Phase 4 conclusion.

The second of the MCU's new special presentations, The Holiday Special, succeeds in achieving all a special should: being entertaining without being unduly related to the main narrative (perhaps replacing the once-popular One Shots).

But it still remains true that the GOTG Holiday Special had a big effect on MCU canon.

The GOTG Holiday Special has a number of incidents that confound viewers since they occur in the MCU chronology.

Others are essentially sad errors that have been made about well-known facts, even in more recent Phase 4 releases.

There are just a few MCU releases that don't need extensive historical study and considerably greater attention to minute details, though, due to the responsibility that comes with creating MCU products nowadays.

However, this is nothing new because the Infinity Gauntlet Easter egg, which had to be changed and repurposed as a joke on Asgard, caused the Infinity Saga to be derailed right from the start. The GOTG Holiday Special has some clear problems, but nothing as blatant.

The Collector's Destiny is Described in the GOTG Holiday Special, But It Causes Issues (But Causes Issues)

The Collector, Taneleer Tivan, was said to have survived his battle with Thanos and had sold the Guardians to Knowhere in the Guardians of the Galaxy Holiday Special.

Benicio Del Toro asserted following the publication of Avengers: Infinity War that he thought The Collector was still alive despite Thanos' assault on Knowhere and forceful appropriation of the Reality Stone.

Since then, rumors have circulated that he may join forces with The Grandmaster (Jeff Goldblum), a mythical brother who was also last seen attending to his wounds following a loss.

Despite all of our efforts, it doesn't appear plausible that Thanos would have let The Collector to live, which gets us to the problems with the Holiday Special.

The Collector's ship is logistically destroyed during Thanos' attack on Knowhere, not to mention the havoc this creates in the Celestial head base.

But what was worse was how Thanos handled Tivan. Thanos expresses his true thoughts towards The Collector by mocking him by tormenting him and showing open contempt for his lack of respect.

The idea of The Collector departing (without a ship) seems completely unlikely given the harm done to Knowhere and the known fact that the Collector is personally enamored with the Infinity Stones.

Even though Thanos doesn't randomly kill people, he killed Loki out of spite. It raises more questions than if he had simply passed away, at the very least.

The Earth Can No Long Recognize The Guardians

The Young Avenger adversary in Ms. Marvel displays her admiration for Earth's Mightiest Heroes in the most comic book fan-friendly situation imaginable: at an Avengers-themed conference.

When Kamala Khan visits AvengerCon, she will unavoidably run across a crowd of cosplayers and a plethora of Avengers merch.

The Avengers are clearly mentioned in the most of the Easter eggs, but there are also some perplexing connections to the Guardians of the Galaxy.

Other items include Rocket Raccoon plush toys, the autobiography of Peter Quill, and incredibly authentic Gamora costumes.

It's obvious that after arriving on Earth and becoming famous after Endgame, the Guardians joined the ranks of the Avengers. Otherwise, they wouldn't have gained such notoriety.

Quill is not even from Earth, so that has never made sense. Because he was not reared there, he is not drawn to it.

The fact that she died and vanished in Infinity War and Endgame, respectively, complicates Ms. Marvel's Gamora cosplay error even more.

The fact that neither Drax nor Mantis get any notice upon their arrival on Earth is resolved in the GOTG Holiday Special while also creating a new one.

It's a nice enhancement, but Ms. Marvel makes it harder to find the other Guardians Easter eggs.

Kingo seems to be back on Earth after Eternals.

Kingo is doing a cheerful one-man show called Kingo's Christmas after returning to Earth from the Eternals, according to backstory information in the GOTG holiday special.

It is being promoted on Hollywood Boulevard as Drax and Mantis look for Kevin Bacon.

The issue is that Kingo was exiled from Earth by Arishem as part of Earth's punishment after the cliffhanger conclusion of The Eternals.

If Kingo returns to Earth, either the heroes who betrayed Arishem were set free and Earth received a passing grade, or something went wrong in the MCU story's fourth act.

The Celestial Judge's abrupt decision to reverse course and permit Kingo to continue his performing career strikes us as extremely odd.

Yondu has always been recognized as Star-father Lord's

In a franchise that is often driven by father concerns, Guardians of the Galaxy Vol. 2's denouement was both unexpected and sad, offering a positive message about unusual parental bonds.

Yondu was always Lord's father, despite the fact that Ego may have been Star-father; when Lord realized this, his imminent death was filled with a horrible agony.

It was especially clever since it changed Peter's perspective of the person he had thought had been his main tormentor.

In the GOTG Christmas special, a flashback cruelly undermined Yondu's resolve. Yondu makes a second appearance in the show's two animated bookends, portraying both sides of the Grinch tale.

He discovered that he shared Peter's enthusiasm for the vacation, so he gave Peter his twin blasters as a first present.

Star-supposed Lord's ignorance of Yondu's role as his adopted father is disproved by the positive footnote, which deprives the subsequent disclosure of its significance.

Bucky No Longer Possesses His Arm...

Rocket Raccoon is presented with Bucky Barnes' arm, the ideal Christmas present, in the closing moments of The Guardians of the Galaxy Holiday Special.

The victory was established as canon for the MCU by James Gunn's account of how Gamora defeated Bucky despite his super soldier powers and vibranium arm.

Bucky's arm is prominently displayed in the first piece of Thunderbolts' official art, which inevitably causes controversy.

Do you truly believe Rocket returned the arm? Did Bucky go into space to find it? Did he continue to obtain vibranium from Wakanda in spite of the increasingly stringent limitations put in place on the most priceless resource in the country, as seen in Wakanda Forever?

Marvel fans are going to ask that type of question, and the GOTG Holiday Special almost has a witty, provocative answer for it.

How Groot ages is a different query that is more of a riddle than a canon one.

Between Groot's phases of being the potted off-cut in the Guardians of the Galaxy credits, the dancing baby Groot stage, and the cranky teenage Groot stage, it feels like only a few months have passed.

That period looks to continue beyond Avengers: Endgame for a further two years, according to Thor: Love & Thunder.

Then, not too long after that (as reasonably suggested by Kraglin's ongoing unfamiliarity with the Yaka arrow), it is said that Groot is in full swole late adolescent/early adult stage.

He is a walking alien tree combatant, therefore The Guardians of the Galaxy Holiday Special may get away with it despite the lack of consistency.

The Bucky's Arm scene has gone popular online.

The show had several noteworthy scenes with Marvel characters. Viewers particularly enjoy the scene where Rocket accepts Bucky's prosthetic limb.

James Gunn wrote and directed the Guardians of the Galaxy Holiday Special, which starred Kevin Bacon, Star-Lord, Mantis, Drax, Rocket, Nebula, Kraglin, Cosmo the Spacedog, and an animated Yondu.

The Avengers: Infinity War joke is finished when Nebula offers Rocket Bucky's Vibranium prosthetic arm.

Rocket questioned Bucky in Avengers: Infinity War while they fought alongside one another in Wakanda because he was impressed by the prosthetic arm.

Please let me know how much the arm costs. It looked like a good time in the middle of the fight.

However, Rocket is a raccoon who enjoys using destructive technology and weapons.

Rocket asks Bucky if he would be interested in buying the arm, but Bucky simply walks away. Rocket ends the scene by saying, "I'll get that arm, you know".

Who would have imagined that Rocket would one day receive Bucky's arm, and that too as a gift?

At least not with The Guardians of the Galaxy Holiday Special, which came as a complete surprise to Marvel fans.

Both Marvel characters originate from underprivileged origins. Amazingly, Rocket's dreadful story and Nebula's are exactly the same.

Rocket observed Nebula being tortured by her perverted and vicious "father" Thanos, as well as the researchers who experimented on the raccoon.

Although Rocket and Groot are depicted as being the best of friends in MCU's Guardians of the Galaxy Vol. 1, Rocket might possibly be closer to Nebula.

Nebula and Rocket have a solid understanding of one another after spending so much time in space together and having a horrific past.

Rocket must have been joking when he said he wanted Bucky's arm. The fact that Nebula took things to heart and asked for the arm for Christmas suggests that she cares deeply for Rocket.

Does Nebula give Rocket the actual Bucky's arm?

The answer to one essential question, however, is still pending: Is the arm Rocket receives from Nebula the real thing, or is it a replica?

The answer, however, cannot be presented in The Guardians of the Galaxy Holiday Special unless we wish to sabotage the scene between Nebula and Rocket.

Let's look at whether the arm was real or made up in the meantime since it may or may not be handled in a future MCU effort.

For those of you who first believed Bucky had two bionic limbs, let's go back in time.

Iron Man injured Bucky's arm, a Dr. Zola creation, during their fight in Captain America: Civil War. That eliminates the titanium arm from consideration, leaving only the Wakandan Vibranium arm.

It's hardly impossible that the arm Bucky obtained from the Wakandans is the one featured in The Guardians of the Galaxy Holiday Special. Nebula would have trouble reaching Bucky's arm, though.

In light of the events of Avengers: Infinity War, Nebula can ask the Wakandans to build her another bionic arm.

It would be odd for Nebula to be around the Wakandans because she hasn't been one to display her emotions.

which just left us with one option. It's probably a replica of the bionic arm that Nebula gifted Rocket for Christmas in The Guardians of the Galaxy Holiday Special.

At least until Marvel Studios verifies whether it was the real deal or not, that's a logical conclusion.

What Character Did James Gunn Reprise for the Guardians of the Galaxy Holiday Special?

James Gunn, the writer and director of the recently released Disney+ special titled "Guardians of the Galaxy Holiday Special," reveals that he reprises a certain role from an earlier Marvel Cinematic Universe film.

Star-Lord (Chris Pratt), Drax (Dave Bautista), Mantis (Pom Klementieff), Rocket (Bradley Cooper), Groot (Vin Diesel), and Nebula (Karen Gillan) are back for a short, holiday-themed adventure before the release of Guardians of the Galaxy Vol. 3 next year.

The program, which lasts for roughly 45 minutes, has won the admiration of viewers and critics alike for its upbeat tone, rocking soundtrack, and unexpected emotional turns.

James Gunn recently revealed that he once again serves as the model for Groot's dance skills in response to a fan's question on Twitter about how Groot was created for The Guardians of the Galaxy Holiday Special.

In two of the special's memorable musical performances, Groot and the other Guardians demonstrate their dance skills.

Gunn previously handled the motion capture for Baby Groot's dancing sequence in the entertaining Guardians of the Galaxy Vol. 2 opening action scene.

Groot's Evolution Throughout the MCU

The first Guardians of the Galaxy film's heartbreaking climax features the death of the original Groot, who was taller and had a deeper voice.

He gave his life to save his comrades. Despite only only saying "I am Groot" in a variety of intonations, the character soon won many fans.

Despite Gunn's confirmation that Groot's original form did indeed perish in Guardians of the Galaxy, a new Groot emerges in Guardians of the Galaxy Vol. 2.

The charming hero, now known as Baby Groot, is no longer the sage and imposing figure from the first film, but rather is playful and naive, and he is a major source of humor in the sequel.

The Guardians of the Galaxy played significant roles in Avengers: Infinity War and Avengers: Endgame, despite not having their own standalone film since 2017.

In the two Avengers films, Groot has a much younger appearance and a more abrasive attitude, which provides for some entertaining exchanges with Rocket.

Additionally, Groot demonstrates his fighting prowess once more in the two films, in contrast to Baby Groot's overall indifference for adversaries in Guardians of the Galaxy Vol. 2.

Groot changes considerably more physically in the Guardians of the Galaxy holiday special. The new Groot, also known as Swoll Groot or YA Groot, is noticeably stockier than the previous Groot was, which may hint at future developments in Guardians of the Galaxy Vol. 3.

Although The Guardians of the Galaxy Holiday Special doesn't explicitly hint at what will happen in the upcoming final episode, Groot's new muscular appearance may indicate that viewers will be seeing the hero transform into a much more potent fighting force.

Gunn has previously hinted that a significant portion of Guardians of the Galaxy Vol. 3 would center on Rocket's terrible past, but as Groot grows stronger and more outspoken, there may also be some intriguing changes in the dynamics of the Guardians of the Galaxy's characters.

References

h ttps://screenrant.com/guardians-galaxy-holiday-special-phase-4-plot-hole/

https://www.thepopverse.com/guardians-of-the-galaxy-holiday-special-the-endings-the-credits-and-more-explained